A Royal Tea

★ Also by ★
Debbie Dadey

MERMAID TALES

BOOK 1: *TROUBLE AT TRIDENT ACADEMY*

BOOK 2: *BATTLE OF THE BEST FRIENDS*

BOOK 3: *A WHALE OF A TALE*

BOOK 4: *DANGER IN THE DEEP BLUE SEA*

BOOK 5: *THE LOST PRINCESS*

BOOK 6: *THE SECRET SEA HORSE*

BOOK 7: *DREAM OF THE BLUE TURTLE*

BOOK 8: *TREASURE IN TRIDENT CITY*

Coming Soon

BOOK 10: *A TAIL OF TWO SISTERS*

Mermaid Tales

Debbie Dadey

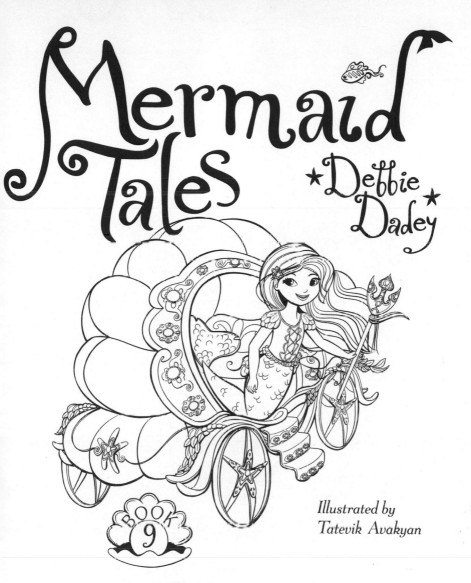

BOOK 9

Illustrated by
Tatevik Avakyan

A Royal Tea

ALADDIN

NEW YORK   LONDON   TORONTO   SYDNEY   NEW DELHI

ALADDIN

An imprint of Simon & Schuster Children's Publishing Division

1230 Avenue of the Americas, New York, NY 10020

First Aladdin hardcover edition August 2014

Text copyright © 2014 by Debbie Dadey

Illustrations copyright © 2014 by Tatevik Avakyan

All rights reserved, including the right of reproduction in whole or in part in any form.

ALADDIN is a trademark of Simon & Schuster, Inc.,

and related logo is a registered trademark of Simon & Schuster, Inc.

Also available in an Aladdin paperback edition.

For information about special discounts for bulk purchases,

please contact Simon & Schuster Special Sales at 1-866-506-1949

or business@simonandschuster.com.

The Simon & Schuster Speakers Bureau can bring authors to your live event.

For more information or to book an event contact the

Simon & Schuster Speakers Bureau at 1-866-248-3049

or visit our website at www.simonspeakers.com.

Book design by Karin Paprocki

The text of this book was set in Belucian Book.

Manufactured in the United States of America 0714 FFG

2 4 6 8 10 9 7 5 3 1

Library of Congress Control Number 2013954324

ISBN 978-1-4814-0255-2 (hc)

ISBN 978-1-4814-0254-5 (pbk)

ISBN 978-1-4814-0256-9 (eBook)

To my mother,
Rebecca Bailey Gibson

★ ★ ★ ★

Acknowledgment

Thanks to the SCBWI. This organization's guidance has spawned many wonderful children's stories.

Contents

Holiday?

"**S**HELLY!" MRS. KARP SAID. "What are you doing here?"

Shelly Siren looked around her third-grade classroom in surprise. It was first thing in the morning at her school, Trident Academy, and the other merstudents were just settling into their desks.

"It's Wednesday," Shelly told her teacher. "It isn't a holiday, is it?"

A merboy named Rocky Ridge swam out of his rock desk toward the classroom doorway. "Holiday? All right! I'm going home!"

Mrs. Karp slapped her white tail on her marble desk. "Not so fast, young merman. It's not a holiday."

Rocky groaned, but Shelly was relieved. She had been afraid she had come to school on the wrong day. Things had been a little mixed up at her shell lately.

"I heard your grandfather has penguin pox, Shelly, and I know it's highly contagious," Mrs. Karp said with a worried look on her face, "so I wasn't sure if you'd be at school today."

"Penguin pox? Eek!" Several kids in the classroom pushed their desks away from Shelly's.

Pearl Swamp put a hand over her nose and squealed, "Mrs. Karp, get her out of here right now before we all die!"

Mrs. Karp frowned. "Pearl, you can't die from penguin pox."

"Maybe not," Rocky said. "But you do get itchy black-and-white bumps all over your body."

"Don't worry." Echo Reef put her arm around Shelly. "She isn't sick." Echo was Shelly's best friend.

Shelly nodded, causing her red hair to swirl in the water around her. "My grandfather became ill after he visited a museum in far-off waters. He's locked away with a nurse to take care of him so I don't catch it. I haven't even seen him in days." Shelly's parents had died when she was very young, so she lived with her grandfather.

"I'm glad you're healthy, Shelly. And I hope your grandfather is well soon too," Mrs. Karp said, turning her attention back to the class. "All right, then. Let's all take our seats and get to work. Today we are starting a new unit on penguins!"

Kiki Coral, the smallest mergirl in the class, leaned over and patted Shelly's hand. "I'm sorry about your grandfather. I hope he gets better soon."

Shelly nodded and tried to listen to the science lesson, but she found it hard to concentrate on her favorite subject. Everyone in the merclass, except for Kiki and Echo, kept their desks scooted far away. They even tucked their tails in tightly beneath them so that they wouldn't accidentally touch Shelly. Pearl held her nose whenever she looked at Shelly. No one wanted to catch the penguin pox!

Shelly felt awful. Why was everyone acting like she had a horrible disease? She was almost glad when Rocky yelled, "Mrs. Karp, look! I need to go home. I have the dreaded penguin pox!"

Everyone in the class gasped, but Shelly knew the spots on Rocky's arms were fake. She'd watched him draw them on with a sea quill and octopus ink.

Mrs. Karp rushed over to Rocky, took one look at the pretend spots, and pointed to the hallway. "Mr. Ridge, please step outside for a little conference."

"*Ooh*," several merboys in the room howled as Rocky slowly followed Mrs. Karp out of the classroom.

"Look at what you've done," Pearl snapped at Shelly. "You've gotten poor Rocky into trouble with your icky disease!"

Poor Rocky? Since when did Pearl care about anyone but herself? Shelly sighed. She had a feeling that this wasn't the end of her penguin pox problems.

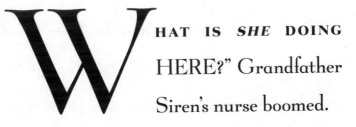

Oh No!

WHAT IS *SHE* DOING HERE?" Grandfather Siren's nurse boomed.

It was after school. Echo and Shelly were enjoying a snack in the kitchen of Shelly's apartment, which was right above Trident City's People Museum.

Shelly wondered if all nurses were as loud as Grandfather's. "Hi, Nurse Bloomquest. This is my best friend, Echo Reef. We're just having some hagfish jelly and lichen crackers," Shelly explained. "Would you like some?"

"*HUMPH.* NO THANKS," Nurse Bloomquest bellowed. "JUST MAKE SURE YOU STAY AWAY FROM YOUR GRANDFATHER'S BEDROOM. IT IS IN QUARANTINE. THAT MEANS NOBODY IN AND NOBODY OUT!"

"Is Grandfather getting any better?" Shelly asked. She knew her grandfather was old for a merman, and she was worried about him.

"HE SHOULD BE AS PERKY AS A SUNFISH SOON ENOUGH," Nurse Bloomquest roared as she left the kitchen.

"That's good news," Echo said as she swallowed the last of her crackers.

Shelly nodded. "I've been trying to keep things clean while he's sick, but I haven't been doing a very good job, as you can probably tell. Nurse Bloomquest makes sure I eat something every day, but she doesn't do any cleaning."

Echo looked at the dirty shells and fish bones scattered around the messy kitchen. She put her right hand on her right hip and grinned. "Maybe you ought to try harder."

"Do you want to help me straighten

up?" Shelly asked. After all, cleaning was always less boring when you shared the work.

Echo nodded. "Sure, but do you mind if we take a quick swim around the People Museum first? I want to see if your grandfather added anything new before he got sick." Shelly's grandfather ran the People Museum, and Echo always liked to browse when she visited Shelly.

Shelly didn't understand her best friend's fascination with everything human, but she sighed and agreed. "Sure, let's go check it out."

The mergirls floated downstairs and into the enormous cavity of the ship that held the museum. Every inch was filled with human objects. A pile of tall, thin pieces of wood that Shelly knew were called oars filled one corner. She thought it must be a pain to have to use oars and a boat to go very far in the ocean.

Shelly scrunched her nose at a pile of stinky, round rubber things with holes in the middle of them. She had no idea what they were used for, but she hated them. For some reason people kept throwing them into the ocean. She'd found more than one dolphin with a black rubber circle stuck around its body!

Echo floated along, looking at the same displays they'd both seen many times before. Some items had little seaweed plaques beside them to describe what they were.

Echo stopped beside a large blue vase sitting on a shelf. "I've always loved this," she said. "Where did your grandfather get it?"

Shelly shrugged. "I'm not sure, but I know he loves it too. He's had it for as long as I can remember. Let me see if there is a description."

But Echo was already examining another human thing. "Is this new?" she asked, picking up a shiny silver object.

As Shelly turned to look, her tail accidentally hit the blue vase. She tried to catch it, but she wasn't fast enough. The vase hit another shelf and broke into ten pieces.

"Oh no!" Shelly squealed.

★ 13 ★

The Queen

THE NEXT MORNING IN CLASS, Pearl scooted her desk closer to Shelly's before tapping Shelly's arm with her gold tail. "Isn't it exciting?" Pearl whispered.

"What?" Shelly asked. She had been so busy worrying about how she could fix her grandfather's vase that she hadn't been paying attention to Mrs. Karp.

And had Pearl actually touched her? Wasn't she still afraid of catching penguin pox?

"Didn't you hear Headmaster Hermit's announcement?" Pearl hissed.

Shelly shook her head and Pearl told her, "Queen Edwina is coming to Trident City tomorrow!"

Shelly was shocked. As far as she knew, Queen Edwina had never been to Trident City before. Plus, Shelly had recently learned that her mother had been a princess, which made Shelly a princess too! In fact, Queen Edwina, the queen of the Western Oceans, was her great-aunt. Shelly's entire class at Trident Academy had also found out that Shelly was a princess, though she wished it was still a secret. All the extra attention made her feel embarrassed.

Shelly had never met any of her royal family, and she was scared to meet the queen. After all, Shelly wasn't exactly a perfect princess. She'd rather play Shell Wars—a fun game where you used whale bones to whack shells—with Rocky than read a *MerStyle* magazine with Pearl. And Shelly loved exploring underwater caves, which often made her dirty with sand and mud. What would the queen think of a dirty princess?

"Mergirls," Mrs. Karp said, giving Shelly and Pearl a disapproving glance.

"Let's pay attention. Queen Edwina loves penguins, so it's wonderful that we're studying them."

Pearl waved her hand in the water. "But, Mrs. Karp, Headmaster Hermit said we should make sure our classrooms are tidy just in case the queen visits our school. Shouldn't we be cleaning up?" Pearl scrunched her nose as she peered around the room.

Mrs. Karp sighed. "I hate to waste valuable learning time, but I suppose we must learn to take care of things too. Let's begin by cleaning our desks."

All around the room merkids began pulling old seaweed homework, sea quills, leftover sea grape snacks, small containers

of octopus ink, and rock
books out of their desks
and putting them into
neat piles or into
the recycling bin.
Rocky's desk was so
stuffed with seaweed
that when he pulled out one piece, hundreds
of little bits exploded all over the classroom.
One small scrap fell into Pearl's hair.

"What is wrong with you?" Pearl snapped
at Rocky, picking the seaweed out of her hair.
"Keep your trash away from me!" Shelly hid
a smile. Unlike yesterday, Pearl didn't seem
to care about "poor" Rocky now.

"Oh no!" Mrs. Karp said, running her
fingers nervously through her green hair.

"Let's get this mess cleaned up!" Echo helped Rocky stuff the jumble into a pot beside his desk.

"Here," Pearl said, giving Shelly a handful of white sand. "Rub your desk with this to make it shine."

Shelly looked at Pearl in surprise. Pearl hardly ever talked to her. She hadn't even invited Shelly to her birthday party this year. But ever since the announcement about Queen Edwina's visit, Pearl was being unusually nice and friendly to Shelly.

"I bet I know why the queen is coming to Trident City," Pearl told Shelly.

"Why?" Shelly asked. She was really curious to know the answer.

"I think she's coming to take you to her

castle," Pearl replied matter-of-factly.

"What?" Shelly said, dropping a blob of white sand on her blue tail.

Pearl nodded. "She heard your grandfather is sick, so she's going to take you away to live with her. You are so lucky! It's a royal rescue!"

Shelly shook her head. "But I don't need rescuing."

"Of course you do," Pearl said. "Your grandfather has penguin pox, for shark's sake! And a princess *can't* get penguin pox. It just wouldn't be proper."

Shelly could barely listen to Pearl go on and on about Neptune's Castle, where the queen lived. Shelly couldn't believe it! Was the queen really going to take her away?

4

Wrong?

I'M NOT GOING TO THE CASTLE," Shelly told Kiki and Echo at lunch later that day. "I don't need to be rescued." The mergirls sat at their usual corner table in the cafeteria with shell bowls full of the day's special, longhorn cowfish.

Kiki took a sip of seaweed juice before shaking her head. "You don't know that the queen is coming to take you away."

"But Pearl said—"

"Since when is Pearl ever right about anything?" Echo interrupted.

Shelly considered this for a minute. Pearl had been wrong when she thought Kiki had stolen her pearl necklace. And she had been wrong when she'd thought that vampire squid were evil. And she had been wrong when she'd thought an old, abandoned ship had pirate treasure on it. Shelly giggled. "You have a point. Pearl isn't an expert at being right."

"But she *is* an expert at causing trouble . . . and here she comes," Echo warned.

Pearl rushed up to their table and gave each mergirl a pickled sea cucumber. "Here, girls, have a little snack."

Shelly wanted to ignore the gift. Who knew what Pearl *really* wanted from her? But Shelly loved sea cucumbers, especially when they were pickled. "Thanks!" she said, quickly popping hers into her mouth before Pearl could change her mind and take it back.

"I've been thinking," Pearl began.

"Oh no," Echo said under her breath.

"I should think the queen will want to stay with you during her visit to Trident City, since you're family and all," Pearl said to Shelly. "But I know your apartment probably isn't fit for royalty."

Shelly's friends gasped. Shelly knew that wasn't a very nice thing for Pearl to say!

But Pearl just kept talking. "Let me know if you need anything. We have lots of fancy stuff at our house you could borrow."

Shelly was so surprised that she nearly

choked on her sea cucumber as Pearl floated away. Kiki patted Shelly on the back until she stopped coughing.

"Do you really think the queen will want to stay with us?" Shelly asked.

Echo shrugged. "The queen *is* your aunt. When my uncle Leopold came to visit, he stayed with us."

Shelly groaned. "But our little apartment isn't ready for the queen! It's not fancy enough." She felt bad even saying those words, but she knew they were true. "Besides, Grandfather has only been sick for three days and I've already made a mess of our whole place!"

Echo nodded. "It *is* pretty messy. I'm sorry I forgot to help you clean yesterday."

"That's okay," Shelly said, shaking her head. "After I broke that vase, I didn't feel like cleaning. But now that the queen is coming, I don't know what I'm going to do! When she sees how untidy and plain things are, she'll definitely want to take me away to live with her."

Echo tossed her sea pickle up in the water. "Don't worry. This is what friends are for. I'll come over after school and help you make your shell sparkle." Echo caught the pickled sea cucumber in her mouth and crunched it.

"You will?" Shelly asked.

Echo nodded. "Of course!"

"I'll help too," Kiki offered. "Everything looks better when it's clean."

When the last conch shell sounded to end the school day, the three mergirls swam to Shelly's apartment. They arrived to find a huge surprise. An enormous shell carriage pulled by two perfectly matched blue dolphins was parked right in front.

"Oh no!" Shelly cried. "We're too late. The queen is already here!"

#
A Royal Announcement

A TALL, THIN MERMAN WITH a large, puffy hat was float-ing near Shelly's apartment door. He bowed low as the girls swam toward him. "Greetings, Princess Shelly and subjects."

Shelly felt her face turn bright red.

She still wasn't used to being called a princess.

"Hello," she said timidly. "Is my aunt, Queen Edwina, here?"

"Of course not. If she were here, there would be many more servants. I am simply here to bring you an announcement," the tall merman said.

Shelly let out a sigh of relief, but Echo asked, "What is the announcement?"

The merman pulled out a large scroll of seaweed. He unrolled it and read in a loud voice, "Queen Edwina requests the pleasure of tea with her niece Princess Shelly on the morrow. Her Royal Highness, Queen of the Western Oceans, will arrive at the Siren apartment shortly after the last Trident Academy conch shell sounds. Her majesty's schedule allows her exactly one hour to visit."

"Here?" Shelly asked with a squeak.

"Here." The merman nodded, rolling up the scroll. He bowed once and then quickly floated into the waiting carriage. The large dolphins pulled the carriage away quicker than a John Dory fish can swallow its dinner.

Shelly was glad that the queen wouldn't be *staying* at her apartment, but now she had something new to worry about. "What

am I going to do?" she wailed. "Grandfather is still sick, and I don't even know
how to *make* tea!"

"Don't worry," Kiki reassured her. "I
can make a wonderful comb jelly tea using
a recipe from my family in the Eastern
Oceans. It's not fancy, but it's very tasty."

"And we'll help you make food, too,"
Echo added.

Shelly hugged them both. "You are the
best merfriends in the entire merkingdom."

"First things first. Let's get to cleaning," Echo said. "Kiki and I will scrub the
kitchen. You start on the rest of the apartment."

Echo swept fish scales off the floor of
Shelly's kitchen, and Kiki used cleaner

wrasse to get rid of the crumbs on the rock counter. Shelly swished around a feather-star duster to make the furniture sparkle. Everything was put in its right place, and the apartment looked shiny and clean. Shelly smiled. Maybe the queen's visit would go smoothly after all.

But then she remembered the broken vase in the museum. She swam downstairs with her friends to show them the shattered pieces.

"Grandfather is going to be so upset that I broke his favorite vase, he might just *want* me to move in with Queen Edwina!" Shelly moaned.

"Don't be silly," Kiki said. "Accidents happen."

"I have an idea! I'll ask my dad," Echo suggested. "Maybe he has some glue in the store that can fix broken vases." Echo's family owned Reef's Store, a place where merfolk could buy nearly anything.

"Really?" Shelly said.

"Sure! Let's go ask him right now," Echo told her. "We'll get this vase fixed up in no time. Your grandfather will never even know it was broken!"

Shelly breathed a sigh of relief. She sure hoped Echo was right!

Emperor

THAT'S TERRIBLE!" PEARL snapped the next day in class. "The queen should visit Trident Academy. After all, we're the most prestigious school in the whole merkingdom."

Mrs. Karp peered at the class through

her tiny glasses. "That may be true, but Queen Edwina has a very busy schedule. Perhaps she will see us on her next visit."

"But I wanted to meet the queen!" Pearl grumbled. "I cleaned my desk and polished my tail for nothing."

"The good news is that since the queen won't be visiting our school, we can concentrate on our study of penguins," Mrs. Karp said with a smile. "Who can tell me the name of the world's largest penguin?"

Kiki raised her hand and called out, "The emperor penguin."

"Very good," Mrs. Karp said. "One interesting fact about emperor penguin males is that they keep their eggs on top of their feet for two months."

"Pee-ew! I bet those eggs stink," Rocky said, holding his nose.

A merboy named Adam asked, "How do they keep from breaking the eggs?"

"They don't move," Mrs. Karp explained. "All the males huddle together and protect the eggs with their feathery skin. By the time the eggs hatch, the fathers have lost half their body weight because they don't eat during that entire time."

"That's the craziest thing I've ever heard!" Rocky said. "Who could sit still for two months?"

"Good thing Rocky isn't an emperor penguin," Echo said with a giggle.

Shelly had to smile. Rocky had a hard time sitting still for two merminutes.

Of course, today Shelly was the one who couldn't concentrate in class. She was exhausted. She had stayed up very late the night before, putting the pieces of the blue vase back together with the sandcastle worm glue that Mr. Reef had given her.

Now that the vase was fixed, all she could think about was the queen's visit. Echo and Kiki were probably right about the royal rescue. But what if they were wrong? What if the queen *did* try to make her live at Neptune's Castle? Pearl had been right about the queen visiting Shelly's apartment. Maybe Pearl was right about the royal rescue, too!

"Now, who can name another type

of penguin?" Mrs. Karp asked, interrupting Shelly's thoughts. Shelly tried to remember the seventeen they'd read about yesterday, but she couldn't even think of one. Shelly tapped her tail nervously on the floor, hoping Mrs. Karp wouldn't call on her.

As the school day went on, Shelly felt worse and worse. At lunch, she couldn't eat a bite of octopus legs— even though they came with sea-snail mucus dipping sauce, one of her favorites. By the time the last conch shell sounded at the end of the day, Shelly was so nervous that she felt like throwing up. What would happen when Queen Edwina came? What would she think of Shelly? And would the queen really take Shelly away from her grandfather?

Teatime

"I CAN'T DO THIS!" SHELLY TOLD HER friends after school. "I'm not ready for the queen."

They stood in the huge front entrance hall of Trident Academy. A large chandelier of glowing jellyfish lit up colorful ceiling carvings that showed the merpeople's history. Students in third through tenth grades swam past them on their way home. Nearby, a fourth-grade mergirl giggled with Pearl over the most recent issue of *MerStyle* magazine.

"Of course you can!" Echo reassured her. "After all, you are a Trident Academy student. You can do anything!"

Kiki nodded. "And we'll be there with you all the way."

Shelly smiled at her friends and took a deep breath. She was really scared about the queen's visit—especially the thought of being taken away from Trident City—but she was grateful for Kiki and Echo's help. "Okay, I'll try," Shelly said. "But I won't be able to get through it without you."

Echo grinned. "All right, let's go have tea with the queen!"

Shelly tried to think brave thoughts as they swam through MerPark on the way to her apartment, but the closer they got, the more scared she became.

Kiki must have read her mind, because she gave Shelly's hand a little squeeze. "Don't worry. It's natural to be afraid when you don't know what's going to happen, but I have a feeling everything will be okay."

"Did you have a vision?" Shelly asked hopefully. Kiki was one of the few mer-girls who had the gift of sometimes seeing the future. Maybe Kiki knew what would happen today!

But Kiki shook her head, pushing her long black hair out of her face. "No, I didn't have a vision. It's just a feeling I have."

When they arrived at Shelly's apartment, Echo took the glittering plankton bow out of her own hair and put it in Shelly's. "Here, why don't *you* wear this?"

"You look so pretty," Kiki said to Shelly. "Like the prettiest princess in the entire merkingdom!"

"I sure wish grandfather was well so he could be here too," Shelly said sadly. "He's still in quarantine. At least Nurse Bloomquest told me he was much better this morning before she left." Nurse Bloomquest had taken the afternoon off, so she wouldn't be there to greet the queen.

"Speaking of your grandfather, did the glue work?" Echo asked.

Shelly led her merfriends downstairs to the People Museum and stopped in front of the patched vase. "What do you think?" she asked.

The three mergirls stared at the big cracks in the vase where Shelly had pieced it back together.

"It's not . . . *too* bad," Kiki lied.

"Maybe your grandfather won't notice," Echo said brightly.

Shelly's heart sank. She knew her friends were trying to be nice. The glued-together vase had looked fine last night when she was tired, but in the daylight it was easy to see the cracks. Her grandfather would surely notice right away.

Kiki put her arm around Shelly. "Don't worry about that now."

Echo nodded and led the mergirls back upstairs to Shelly's apartment. "Let's get ready for tea. We can work on the vase some more later."

Shelly took a deep breath and helped her friends set out food. The hagfish jelly sandwiches were a little soggy, and the comb jelly tea looked more like sand than jelly. Shelly was afraid that Queen Edwina would be used to fancier food, but she didn't tell Echo and Kiki. After all, they had been so nice to help her when she needed it.

Still, when the mergirls heard a knock at the door, Shelly gasped. Were they *really* ready for the queen?

8

Surprise!

"OH MY NEPTUNE!" PEARL exclaimed. "It's a good thing I came."

"What are you doing here?" Echo asked as Pearl rushed into Shelly's apartment.

Pearl looked around and shook her head. "I'm here to help, of course. Why, I'm even risking getting a horrible disease to come to your aid."

"Help?" Shelly asked. Pearl didn't seem like the kind of mergirl who'd ever want to get her hands dirty.

"I overheard you talking about the queen coming to your apartment, so I rushed to my shell and gathered everything you need for a royal visit," Pearl said. She began unloading small objects from a raft floating behind her.

"Don't worry. Echo and I have already helped Shelly get ready for the queen," Kiki told Pearl.

"Do you have flowers?" Pearl asked.

"Um, no," Shelly said.

"You *must* have flowers!" Pearl said,

pushing a bouquet of sea lavender into Shelly's arms. "Give these to the queen when she arrives. It's a tradition, and these are her favorite."

"How do you know that?" Kiki asked.

Pearl rolled her eyes. "I read!"

Shelly didn't know where in the ocean Pearl had read that, but she was grateful as Pearl put fancy seaweed napkins, a centerpiece of beach morning glories, and some delicious-looking food on the table. Oysters in moon jellyfish mucus, feathery pulse coral cookies, and honeycomb worm scones were stacked on gleaming golden plates.

"Thanks, but we already have food," Echo said.

Pearl sniffed at the hagfish jelly sandwiches. "A little extra food couldn't hurt. Here's some coconut milk to have with your tea. I could have brought more if you'd told me about this yesterday."

"This is really nice of you, Pearl," Shelly admitted.

Pearl winked. "I know how to handle these royals. After all, I've read every issue of *MerStyle* magazine for the last two years."

When they were finished, Shelly couldn't believe how wonderful the apartment looked. Every corner sparkled, and the kitchen table was overflowing with fresh flowers and delicious-looking snacks.

"I was so nervous earlier," she told the mergirls. "But thanks to you, I'm feeling better."

Pearl nodded. "Now, here's what you do. Never touch the queen. Make sure you call her Your Majesty. Don't sit or eat until she does. Put your napkin in your lap. And be sure to curtsy when you first meet her."

Shelly's head was spinning with all of Pearl's instructions. She was glad when Echo asked, "What does 'curtsy' mean?"

Pearl's eyes grew wide. "What would you do without me?" Pearl showed them how to twist their fins and bend in a curtsy. When Echo, Shelly, and Kiki tried it, they all fell over.

"Keep practicing," Pearl commanded.

"Especially you, Shelly. After all, the queen is coming to rescue you!"

Echo frowned. "What are you talking about?"

"Queen Edwina is taking Shelly to live with her at Neptune's Castle," Pearl explained. "She's saving her from catching the icky penguin pox!"

Kiki shook her head. "That's not true, Pearl!"

Pearl opened her mouth to argue just as a trumpet fish horn blared from outside.

"Oh no!" Shelly squealed. "She's here!" Her tummy felt like it was doing tail flips!

9

Queen Edwina

OUTSIDE THE PEOPLE Museum, a crowd of mer-folk had gathered around a sparkling shell carriage that was pulled by a large killer whale. Two tailmen wearing bright blue coats with silver sashes lowered

a glittering step from the carriage onto the ocean floor.

"I think that step is made of diamonds," Pearl whispered. All four mergirls stared in wonder as another tailman, also wearing a blue coat, but with a gold sash, said in a loud voice, "Announcing the arrival of Her Royal Majesty, Queen of the Western Oceans, Guardian of the Mid-Atlantic Ridge, and Patron of All Basin Life."

"That's some name," Echo murmured with a nervous giggle.

The tailman continued, "From the ancient lineage of Cronus, all hail the Keeper of the Western Trident, Queen Edwina the Wonderful."

Another conch shell sounded, and a different tailman opened the carriage door. Out floated a small, round merwoman with bright red hair, wearing a crown of glittering jewels. Queen Edwina held a gleaming trident in one hand and a small golden box in another.

"Thank you, Thatcher," the queen said. "That will be all." Quickly the tailman retreated, and the queen floated forward. The servants stood between the crowd and the queen. The queen nodded toward the crowd.

"Long live Queen Edwina!" an old merman shouted.

Many Trident Academy teachers were in the crowd, including Mrs. Karp. Shelly was surprised to see her. The merpeople waved and cheered at their queen.

Shelly's throat became tight with fear. She knew she should say something to her aunt, but she couldn't seem to find her voice.

As if Pearl could read minds, she tapped Shelly's shoulder and whispered, "Curtsy."

All four girls managed wobbly curtsies, and Shelly thrust the bouquet of sea lavender toward the queen.

"How lovely," Queen Edwina said. "These are my favorite."

Pearl smiled. "Your Majesty, may I hold the box for you?"

"Thank you," Queen Edwina said with a smile. Pearl took the golden box so the queen could accept the flowers from Shelly.

Shelly's heart raced. She didn't know what to say. Kiki and Echo stared at the queen with big eyes.

Luckily, Pearl knew what to do. "Ma'am, may I introduce Princess Shelly and her loyal merfriends Kiki and Echo."

Each of the girls curtsied when Pearl called her name.

"I am your humble servant Pearl." Pearl made a grand curtsy, and her long strand of pearls swept the ocean floor.

Echo, Kiki, and Shelly quickly looked at Pearl with surprise. "Humble" was never a word that Shelly would use to describe Pearl. And Pearl certainly would *not* want to be someone's servant!

"It is lovely to meet all of you," Queen

Edwina said to them, but she was really staring at Shelly. "And, Princess Shelly, how is your grandfather? I understand he has the penguin pox."

Shelly didn't want to tell the queen he was still sick, so she quickly replied, "He is almost fully recovered."

The queen smiled. "I am so glad."

"May we offer Your Royal Highness some tea?" Pearl asked.

Now Shelly was mad at herself. *She* should have been the one to offer the queen tea. *She* should have been the one talking to the queen, not Pearl.

"That would be delightful," Queen Edwina said. "And afterward, I'd love a private word with Princess Shelly. I have something important to discuss with her."

Sweet seaweed! Shelly's heart stopped. Was the queen going to ask her to leave her home in Trident City?

Something Unpleasant

WHAT A LOVELY PLANK-
ton bow you are wear-
ing," Queen Edwina
told Shelly. Echo, Kiki, Pearl, Shelly, and
the queen were all seated around the table
in Shelly's small kitchen.

"And this tea is wonderful," Queen

Edwina added. "I haven't had any like it since my last trip to the Eastern Oceans."

"Echo lent me her bow, and Kiki made the tea," Shelly told her great-aunt. Kiki and Echo smiled.

Pearl cleared her throat. Shelly said, "And the flowers and snacks came from Pearl."

"Except for the jelly sandwiches," Pearl said quickly.

The queen nodded. "Shelly, it appears you have very thoughtful merfriends here in Trident City. It has been such a treat to meet them, but now I require a private audience with you."

The queen picked up the golden box that Pearl had placed on the table.

"We'll be outside if you need anything," Echo whispered in Shelly's ear. Kiki, Pearl, and Echo waved good-bye as they floated out of the room.

Shelly gulped as they left. Would she ever see them again, or would the queen whisk her away to Neptune's Castle? The very thought of leaving her friends behind gave Shelly a burst of courage.

"I really love living here," she said. "I'm sorry that Grandfather is not feeling well enough to greet you himself, but the nurse told me that his quarantine will be over later today."

The queen nodded. "That is good news. But now I must talk about something that might be unpleasant for you to hear."

Shelly's heart pounded and tears filled her eyes. The queen seemed nice enough, but Shelly didn't want to leave her home.

"I am sorry I have not visited you since your parents' death," Queen Edwina began. "But I am glad you had a normal fryhood instead of being brought up as a princess. Your mother, Princess Lenore, would have wanted it that way. She was a wonderful merlady. Her sweet laugh was like sea bells tinkling with the tide."

"You knew my mother?" Shelly asked softly. Shelly's parents had died when she was so young that she'd never really known them.

"Of course. She was my sister's daughter." Queen Edwina handed Shelly the golden box. "In fact, I've collected some mementos of your mother in here. I thought you might like to have them."

Shelly touched the fancy design engraved into the top of the box. A big letter *L* was surrounded by a crown. With her merheart pounding, she slowly opened the box and lifted out a golden necklace. Two faces had been carved into the shell pendant. Shelly gasped. One face looked much like her own!

"That's your mother and father. Your mother was beautiful, just like you," Queen Edwina said. "There are also some seaweed letters in the box, but you can read those in private. Your father wrote them to your mother when they were first engaged."

"Thank you," Shelly said, holding the necklace and box close. Her heart fluttered, knowing she actually had something that her mother had touched. She didn't own anything else that had belonged to her parents. "I will treasure these always."

"I was concerned that they might upset you," Queen Edwina explained. "Some people find it painful to talk of those who are no longer with us."

Shelly shook her head. "No, I like to hear about my parents." In fact, she often wished her grandfather would talk about them more. Now she realized that maybe it was a hard topic for him to discuss. After all, her father had been his son.

"Now, about Neptune's Castle . . . ," Queen Edwina began.

Before she could stop herself, Shelly blurted, "Oh no! Please don't make me live there. I'm sure it is very nice, but I want to stay here with Grandfather Siren and my friends."

Queen Edwina laughed. "Well, I am sure you do. I was merely going to suggest that you might visit me during your school break. You could see your parents' quarters in the castle and meet the rest of your royal family."

Shelly was shocked. "So you didn't come to take me away?" she asked.

"No, of course not," the queen told her. "You seem to be doing quite well here in Trident City. But I do require one more thing from my grandniece before I leave."

The Royal Castle

SHELLY DIDN'T KNOW WHAT else the queen could want. "Would you like some more tea?" she asked, reaching for the pot.

"No thank you, but I *would* like a hug," Queen Edwina said.

Shelly laughed and gave her great-aunt a

giant squeeze. All her worries melted away in the queen's warm embrace. It seemed that Pearl had been wrong about two more things: Shelly's great-aunt hadn't come to take her away, and sometimes it *was* okay to touch the queen.

"Now, I'm afraid I must be off to attend to my royal duties," her aunt told her.

"Is it hard to be a queen?" Shelly asked. As difficult as it was for her to believe, it was entirely possible that someday Shelly could be queen herself. Her grandfather had told her that she was third in line for the crown.

"Sometimes it's not easy," Queen Edwina said with a nod. "But I do like being able to help less fortunate merfolk by raising money through my mercharities. It's most important to try to be honest and caring."

Shelly followed her great-aunt as she glided toward the glistening royal carriage. Echo, Pearl, and Kiki met them just outside the door, and all four girls stared at the carriage's brilliant jewels. The crowd of Trident City mercitizens cheered when the queen appeared. Now they were held back by a golden rope and several Shark Patrol guards. The three tailmen immediately assisted Queen Edwina. One opened the carriage door and extended a gloved hand to help the queen.

Shelly's great-aunt turned and waved before entering the carriage. "Good-bye, Princess Shelly. Please visit me soon."

Pearl gasped at the Queen's next words: "And your friends are welcome too."

Kiki, Echo, and Shelly waved as the queen left. It wasn't until the carriage had disappeared into the murky water that the girls noticed that Pearl hadn't been waving along with them. She had fainted!

Kiki crouched down and fanned Pearl's face. "Pearl! Pearl! Are you all right?" she asked.

Pearl sat up with a dazed look on her face. "Of course I'm all right! Did you hear that? We're invited to the royal castle. I have to make sure I have something to wear!" Before anyone could speak, Pearl sped off toward her shell.

"Whew!" Echo said. "Shelly, you did it!"

"And the queen didn't take you away!" added Kiki.

Shelly hugged her friends. "I couldn't have made it through without you both. Thanks for all your help."

Just then they heard a shuffling sound from inside the apartment. "Shelly!" her grandfather yelled. "Where did all this food come from? Did you have a party without me?"

Shelly froze. She was glad her grandfather was up and walking around, but what about the broken vase? What would she tell him?

12

Pox Free

SO, IS YOUR GRANDFATHER all better now?" Echo asked the next morning. The two girls floated past a statue of Poseidon in MerPark on their way to school.

"Yes, he is totally penguin-pox free," Shelly said with relief.

The night before, Grandfather Siren had even felt well enough to munch on some of the leftover snacks while Shelly told him all about the royal visit.

"Guess which treat he liked best?" Shelly asked.

Echo shrugged. "One of Pearl's fancy creations?"

Shelly shook her head. "No wavy way. He thought your hagfish jelly sandwiches were delicious."

Echo giggled. "Don't tell Pearl. She'd be furious."

"That's true, but it was nice of her to help."

Shelly was still pretty surprised that Pearl had braved the penguin pox to help her. And honestly, she didn't know what she would have done without Pearl's advice. Shelly would be sure to invite Pearl to come with her, Kiki, and Echo to visit Neptune's Castle during their school vacation.

"Did he find out about the vase?" Echo said. "I wish we'd had more time to fix it."

Shelly nodded. "He was upset. At first he thought maybe the queen's servants had broken it by accident."

"Did you tell him the truth?" Echo asked.

"I did," Shelly said, remembering Queen Edwina's advice about being honest and caring. "And Grandfather told me my father had found the vase on a trip long ago. That's why it was so important to Grandfather Siren."

Echo stopped floating. "It was his special way of remembering his son?"

"Yes," Shelly said. A little tear slid from her eye as she thought about the father she'd never known. "But guess what? Grandfather Siren said that he has something much better to remember his son by."

"What's that?" Echo asked.

"Me!" Shelly said with a smile.

"You *are* the best!" Echo said as they floated past another statue in MerPark. "But I bet your grandfather was sorry he missed the queen."

"He laughed and said, 'What a coincidence,'" Shelly told her friend.

Echo frowned. "Why?"

"Well, you know Grandfather had the penguin pox," Shelly explained.

Echo nodded. "Everyone knows that."

"Yes, but can you guess what picture Queen Edwina's royal carriage has on its side?" Shelly asked.

Echo giggled. "Are you kidding?"

"Nope, Queen Edwina *loves* penguins!" Shelly told her friend.

"I bet her favorite is the emperor penguin!" Echo laughed.

Shelly grinned. She was pretty lucky. Sure, she might not feel like a real princess sometimes. But great friends could make anyone feel like royalty!

Class Reports

* ★ *

KING PENGUIN

By Shelly Siren

The king penguins do not build nests for their eggs. The mother and father take turns holding their egg on their feet, like the emperor penguin.

MACARONI PENGUIN
By Echo Reef

Macaroni penguins have funny yellow markings above their eyes that meet on their foreheads. They lay two eggs a year, and both parents take care of the eggs.

AFRICAN PENGUIN
By Rocky Ridge

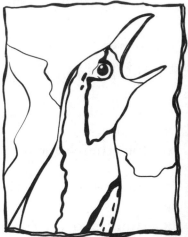

This penguin makes a strange braying sound. Humans sometimes destroy their nests and ruin their homes. Guess why the people do it? They want penguin poop for making their crops grow! How weird is that?

LITTLE PENGUIN

By Pearl Swamp

The little penguin is the smallest of all the penguins. It leaves the water only at night. Most penguins are strange-looking, with their big white chests, but the little penguin is cute!

CHINSTRAP PENGUIN

By Kiki Coral

This penguin really does look like it has a strap on its chin. Chinstraps can swim very fast and even leap out of the water like a porpoise. They eat krill.

The Mermaid Song Tales

REFRAIN:

Let the water roar

Deep down we're swimming along

Twirling, swirling, singing the mermaid song.

VERSE 1:

Shelly flips her tail

Racing, diving, chasing a whale

Twirling, swirling, singing the mermaid song.

VERSE 2:

Pearl likes to shine

Oh my Neptune, she looks so fine

Twirling, swirling, singing the mermaid song.

VERSE 3:

Shining Echo flips her tail

Backward and forward without fail

Twirling, swirling, singing the mermaid song.

VERSE 4:

Amazing Kiki

Far from home and floating so free

Twirling, swirling, singing the mermaid song.

Author's Note

MY GRANDMOTHER Gibson used to say our family was related to Francis Scott Key, the man who wrote "The Star-Spangled Banner." I did a little research and found out she was right.

But my research didn't stop there. I kept digging and found out something very strange: I am related to royalty! My ancestors were kings and queens of France, England, and Sweden. But I was most surprised when I found out that my direct ancestor was Cleopatra, a famous ruler of ancient Egypt.

Has your grandmother ever mentioned that you are related to someone famous? Just think, your aunt might be a queen too!

Hope you'll visit the Mermaid Tales pages of debbiedadey.com for some mermaid tea party fun!

From a lost princess,
Debbie Dadey

Glossary

BEACH MORNING GLORY: This coastal flower grows on many islands and on six continents.

CLEANER WRASSE: This silvery blue fish has a black band down its side. It "cleans" other fish by eating parasites and dead tissue right off their skin. It sometimes even cleans divers!

COCONUT: The inside of the coconut fruit contains a tasty coconut milk. Coconuts grow on land, but sometimes they fall into the ocean.

COMB JELLY: The comb jelly was accidentally put into the Black Sea. It is causing trouble for the fishermen there because it eats fish eggs. This makes for far fewer fish.

CONCH: These large sea-snail shells are sometimes used for decoration.

DOLPHINS: The Risso's dolphin, also known as a gray dolphin, can dive for up to a half hour.

FEATHER STAR: The tropical species of feather star has about a hundred arms!

HAGFISH: This long fish ties itself in knots and squeezes out slime!

HONEYCOMB WORM: This tiny creature builds large sand tubes that look like honeycombs.

JELLYFISH: There are many different types of jellyfish. Some of them glow!

JOHN DORY: The John Dory is a very thin fish that can shoot out its jaw and swallow its food quickly.

KILLER WHALE: This black-and-white creature is not a whale, but a dolphin.

LICHEN: When algae and fungus grow together, they can form a compound organism called lichen. If you see orange spots on rocks near the sea, they could be encrusting lichens.

LONGHORN COWFISH: This fish has very long, fleshy horns above its eyes.

OCTOPUS: A giant octopus squirts out purple ink when it's frightened.

OYSTERS: Oysters have been eaten by people for many years. In some waters they have almost vanished.

PENGUIN: This marine bird cannot fly.

PLANKTON: Plankton are small animals that float freely on the surface of the ocean.

PULSE CORAL: This soft coral constantly

opens and closes its feathery tentacles.

SANDCASTLE WORM: This creature uses glue from an organ on its head to put together sand and bits of shell to make its house.

SEA CUCUMBER: This creature crawls along the ocean floor, eating mud. It is almost colorless, but it glows!

SEA LAVENDER: Common sea lavender is a flower that grows near the coast.

SEAWEED: There are many different types of seaweed. Cactus seaweed looks like a mini underwater cactus. Kelp is a type of seaweed.

SUNFISH: Ocean sunfish drift on the surface of the water, looking for floating jellyfish to eat.

VAMPIRE SQUID: This is the only squid that spends its entire life in deep water.

FIND OUT WHAT HAPPENS IN THE NEXT . . .

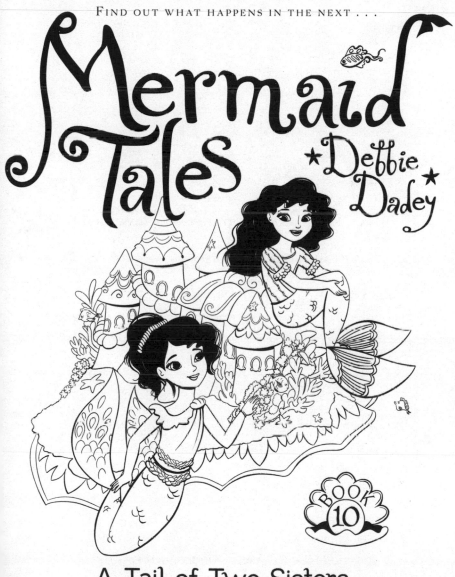

Mermaid Tales

★Debbie Dadey★

BOOK 10

A Tail of Two Sisters

Too Many Tail Flips!

ECHO REEF TUCKED IN HER fins and flipped two times in a row.

"That was tails down the best flip I've ever seen!" Shelly Siren told her. The girls floated outside Echo's shell in the early morning before school.

Echo grinned as she stretched her pink tail. "Thanks! I've been practicing a lot lately. The Tail Flippers are performing a new routine for Parent Night, and Coach Barnacle wants it to be perfect. If anyone misses even one practice, they won't be able to perform!"

The Tail Flippers was their school's gymnastics and dance group. Echo was thrilled that she had made the team this year, and she couldn't wait to show off her new moves on Parent Night.

Echo and Shelly were in the third grade at Trident Academy, a prestigious school for third through tenth graders. They both lived close to the school, but merstudents from faraway waters lived in the dorms.

Many families would be crossing the ocean to visit for Parent Night. Besides the Tail Flippers, the Pep Band and the Trident Chorus would perform, and there would even be a student art show.

"Coach Barnacle wants the Shell Wars team to play a scrimmage that night too," Shelly said. "It will be strange playing in front of so many merpeople." Shell Wars was a game where players took turns whacking shells with whalebones. Echo knew that Shelly was proud to be part of the team.

Echo grinned. "I've never flipped in front of so many merpeople before! It sounds so exciting." Like Shelly, Echo was used to performing in front of her fellow mer-students, but not strangers.

"I just know you'll be totally wavy!" Shelly said.

"Maybe I'd better practice even more," Echo said. "There are only a few days left before Parent Night."

Echo's sister, Crystal, stuck her head out of a window of their family's shell. "Echo, you'd better hurry. It's almost time for school."

Crystal had the same dark hair and eyes as Echo, but she was two years older. Crystal stared at Echo's sparkly T-shirt. "Hey! Isn't that my shirt you're wearing?"

Echo groaned. Lately Crystal was always telling her what to do.

"No, it used to be yours," Echo told her. "Mom gave it to me because it doesn't fit you anymore. And I'm just going to do one more flip."

"Fine," Crystal replied, "but don't blame me if you're late." She paused. "Oh, hi, Shelly. I like your necklace."

Shelly waved. "Thanks. Yours is pretty too."

With that, Crystal swam off in a burst of bubbles.

Debbie Dadey

is the author and coauthor of more than
one hundred and fifty children's books,
including the series The Adventures of the
Bailey School Kids. A former teacher and
librarian, Debbie and her family split their
time between Bucks County, Pennsylvania,
and Sevierville, Tennessee. She hopes
you'll visit www.debbiedadey.com for lots
of mermaid fun.